I WON'T EAT THAT

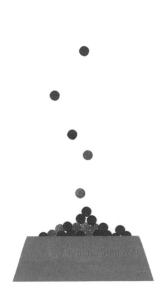

Christopher Silas Neal

WALKER BOOKS
AND SUBSIDIARIES
LONDON · BOSTON · SYDNEY · AUCKLAND

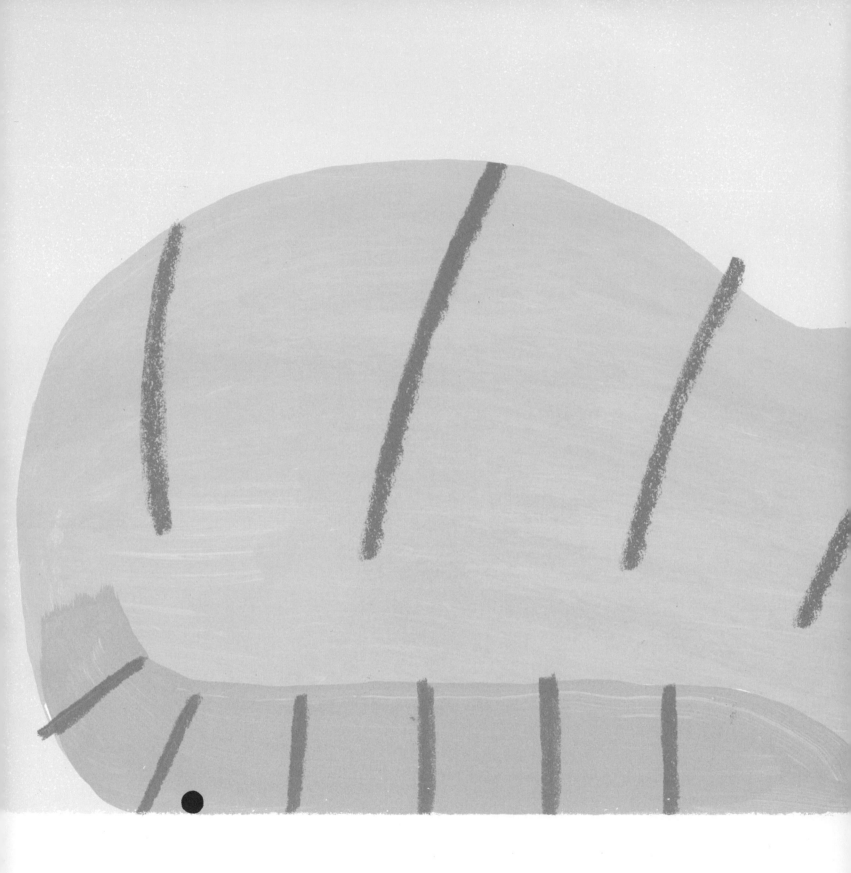

Dogs eat dog food.
Fish eat fish food.

But I'm a cat,
and I will NOT eat cat food.

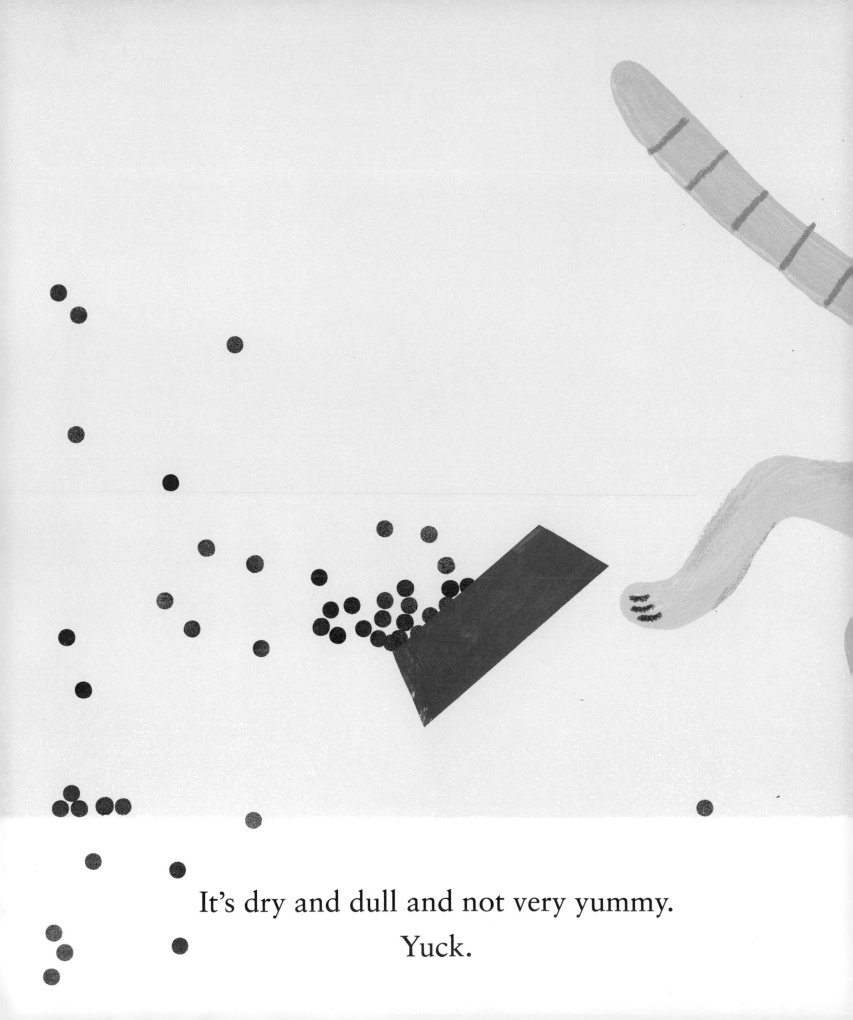

It's dry and dull and not very yummy.
Yuck.

But if I don't eat cat food,
what will I eat?

"Hello, Tortoise.

I'm hungry and searching
for something yummy to eat.

What does a tortoise eat?"

"Worms, of course.
But I must warn you, they wiggle."

"Eww. No, thank you."

"Hello, Fox.

I'm hungry and searching
for something yummy to eat that
doesn't wiggle.

What does a fox eat?"

"Rabbits," replied Fox, as he pounced
on a furry, long-eared critter.
"But I must warn you, they bounce."

"Whoa."

"Hello, Chimp.

I'm hungry and searching
for something yummy to eat that
doesn't wiggle
or bounce.

What does a chimp eat?"

"Ants," replied Chimp. "We use sticks to get them out of trees.
But I must warn you, they bite."

"Yikes! I won't eat that!"

"Lion, please help.

I'm hungry and searching
for something yummy to eat that
doesn't wiggle,
bounce,
or bite.

What does a lion eat?"

"Zebras!" roared Lion, as he sprang after his striped prey.
"But I must warn you—"

"Never mind. There is NO WAY
I'm eating one of those."

"Excuse me, Elephant.

I'm so very hungry and searching
for something yummy to eat that
doesn't wiggle,
bounce,
or bite
and that isn't too big.

What does an elephant eat?"

"Lots and lots of grass.
But I must warn you, it's a little dry."

"Ugh. That's even MORE BORING
than cat food."

"Hey, Whale! Up here!

I'm really hungry and searching
for something yummy to eat that
doesn't wiggle,
bounce,
or bite
and that isn't too big,
too dry,
or too boring.

What does a whale eat?"

"My food is perfect," sang Whale.
"It's none of those things, and it certainly isn't boring.
In fact, my food glows in the dark.

"But I must warn you, it's hard to pronounce.
It's called bioluminescent phytoplankton."

Phyto-what? Whale's food is too weird.
Isn't there anything yummy for me to eat?

"Hi, Cat," squeaked Mouse.
"I'm hungry and searching for something yummy to eat.
What does a cat eat?"

"Hmm ...
I think I've just figured it out.
But I must warn you..."